RETRO LIFESTYLE

WHEN DREAMS TAKE AN UGLY TURN

Volume I

Written and Illustrated by:

ZAHID NAYANI

INDIA • SINGAPORE • MALAYSIA

Copyright © Zahid Nayani 2023
All Rights Reserved.

ISBN 979-8-88849-065-5

This book has been published with all efforts taken to make the material error-free after the consent of the author. However, the author and the publisher do not assume and hereby disclaim any liability to any party for any loss, damage, or disruption caused by errors or omissions, whether such errors or omissions result from negligence, accident, or any other cause.

While every effort has been made to avoid any mistake or omission, this publication is being sold on the condition and understanding that neither the author nor the publishers or printers would be liable in any manner to any person by reason of any mistake or omission in this publication or for any action taken or omitted to be taken or advice rendered or accepted on the basis of this work. For any defect in printing or binding the publishers will be liable only to replace the defective copy by another copy of this work then available.

Disclaimer

No part of this publication may be reproduced, distributed, or transmitted in any form or by any means, including photocopying, recording, or other electronic or mechanical methods, without the prior written permission of the publisher, except as permitted by U.S. copyright law.

The plot, titles, characters, illustrations, and events depicted in this production are all fictional. Therefore, no identification with real people (alive or dead), locations, structures, or bodies of works (real or fictional including comic books, illustrated classics or portfolio of photographers) is intended or should be inferred.

Book Cover by Zahid Nayani and Sagar Nambiar

Illustrations by Zahid Nayani

1st Edition

Thank You Note

Thank you for purchasing my book. "Retro Lifestyle" has been my pet project since 2020. I started amid the uncertain COVID times with limited resources.

The sole objective was to come up with a storyline that could be connected with my music video of the same name. I took up the challenge of creating hundred-odd sketches as per the storyboard, which was then put through a stringent screening process.

I hope you've enjoyed the book as much as I did creating it. Please consider leaving your feedback as a review on Amazon. It will inspire me to plan the next batch of volumes, and this time to enlist the participation of more artists to quicken the creative process.

Christ City News

Retro Wagon Spotted

Fans Rejoice!

A TOUR OF THE WAGON MIGHT NOT BE SUCH A BAD IDEA CONSIDERING THE FACT THAT IT DISAPPEARED IN THIN AIR. THE FANS OF THE DISCO SOUL STAR HAVE BEEN WAITING FOR ALMOST FIVE YEARS NOW; HERE'S WHAT OUR SOURCES HAVE FOUND OUT ABOUT THE NEWEST AND THE LONGEST DISAPPEARING ACT.

Article 1

Retro Wagon spotted!!

Fans Rejoice!!

Christ City News

Picture Courtesy: Rockstar Group

IT SEEMED LIKE JUST YESTERDAY WHEN OUT OF NOWHERE

Article 2

The Elusive Superstar Poses with the Band Members

Christ City News

Church Attracts Visitors Thanks To The Disco / Soul Star's Visit

Picture Courtesy: Rockstar Group

Article 3

Church attracts visitors thanks to the Disco/Soul Star's Visit!

Mr. Ives: What does one gotta do to get some sleep around here?

Scene: Just minutes before the concert, Mr. Ives sneaks into the bathroom

Door knocks: Knock! Knock!

Mr. Ives: My past haunts me to this day; nothing has changed!

Scene: Mr. Ives converses with his reflection in the mirror while getting ready for his concert

Christ City News

Picture Courtesy: Rockstar Group

Article 4

Mr. Ives makes his grand entrance on the stage!!

Crowd goes bananas!!

Christ City News

Reports From The First Leg Of The Tour

Picture Courtesy: Rockstar Group

The Atmosphere Is Electrifying To Say The Least

Article 5

Reports from the first leg of the tour!

The atmosphere is electrifying, to say the least!

Christc City News

Two Back To Back Sold Out Shows!

Fan Verdict, An Absolute Entertainer!

Picture Courtesy: Rockstar Group

Article 6

Two back-to-back sold-out shows!

Fan verdict, an absolute entertainer!

Christ City News

Picture Courtesy: Rockstar Group

Available At Your Nearest Stores Now!

Article 7

Greatest hits compilation released in the midst of the tour!

Available at your nearest stores now!

Christ City News

Shoot Out During The Concert! What?
Live Reports From The Incident Coming Your Way!

Picture Courtesy: Rockstar Group

Article 8

Shootout during the concert! Whatttt????

Live reports from the incident coming your way!

Christ City News

Mr. Ives Fatally Shot In An Unfortunate Incident

Picture Courtesy: Rockstar Group

Paparazzi Starts To Feast On The Story. Mr. Ives Rushed To The Nearest Hospital

Article 9

Mr. Ives was fatally shot in an unfortunate incident!

Paparazzi starts to feast on the story. Mr. Ives was rushed to the nearest hospital.

Christ City News

Mr. Ives Survives, Condition Stable

Picture Courtesy: Rockstar Group

The identity of the shooter remains unknown as the officials continue the investigation. The above picture was taken yesterday after Mr. Ives underwent a surgery.

Article 10

Mr. Ives survives, condition is stable.

Christ City News

Mr. Ives Decides To Open Up About The Ongoing Label Issues And Early Life Struggles After The Fatal Incident To A Longtime Friend And A Former Country Musician Turned Industry Critic, Lonzo!

Picture Courtesy: Rockstar Group

Article 11

Mr. Ives decides to open up about the ongoing label issues, and the early life struggles after the fatal incident to a longtime friend and a former country musician turned industry critic, Lonzo!

Dad: We're officially bankrupt!

Story begins

Retro Lifestyle

Somewhere in the crowded streets of Mumbai, young Mr. Ives (birth name: Lucas) and his father, Henry, are seated in the backseat of the autorickshaw.

Mr. Ives: I am not sure if you know this, Lonzo, but I am originally from Mumbai. I often used to accompany my dad to his pawn shop on the weekends. It was on one such ride when he gently broke the news about us being bankrupt. The pawn shop wasn't making enough money, he said, giving me the option to relocate to the country of my choosing as an attempt to secure my future.

Mr. Ives: Christ City in the UK was the only reasonable option. So, without putting in much thought, I decided to get my documentation done, and within a month's time, I was here.

Mr. Ives: Here I was a 23-year old fresh out of college, who knew nothing about living independently and was desperately looking for jobs to help sustain the monthly expenses.

It's worsening!

Mr. Ives: For the first few months, my only goal was to be able to buy myself a reasonable pair of shoes!

Mr. Ives: In a way, it acted as a motivator, as Christ City's biggest soul star, Noah, only had a handful of clothes and a singular pair of shoes, which he wore for most of his performances until he finally met his manager, who bought him his first fancy pair of brogues

Mr. Ives: Now that I have made a name for myself in the entertainment industry, it might seem like I was already pursuing music from a tender age just like the rest.

However, you will be surprised to learn that I had no clue as to what I wanted to do till I saw a bunch of musicians across the tower bridge busking for a living.

Mr. Ives: Amongst the talented bunch playing on the streets, there was this one particular performer who caught my attention, the metal-headed magician, my love, Genine!

Mr. Ives: I used to watch her perform everyday from 5 PM to 7 PM without fail. One fine day, she finally noticed me being her number one cheerleader. As far as spectators were concerned, I was amongst the regulars, probably more excited than anyone else.

One thing led to another, and somehow in the midst of us conversing, she told me about the money that she used to make on holidays and also, why all the musicians occupied the streets of the tower bridge. The minute she told me about minting $1500 in a day, I decided that, I would be a part-time musician. Of course, it was easier said than done.

Mr. Ives: Oh! I forgot to mention my job, but I finally managed to get one. For almost 8 years, I drove dead people in and out of funeral homes.

I was an on-call hearse driver. Driving being the only skill that I possessed, I never thought that out of all the cab services that I had applied for, it would be the private coffin conveying vehicle service that would hire me.

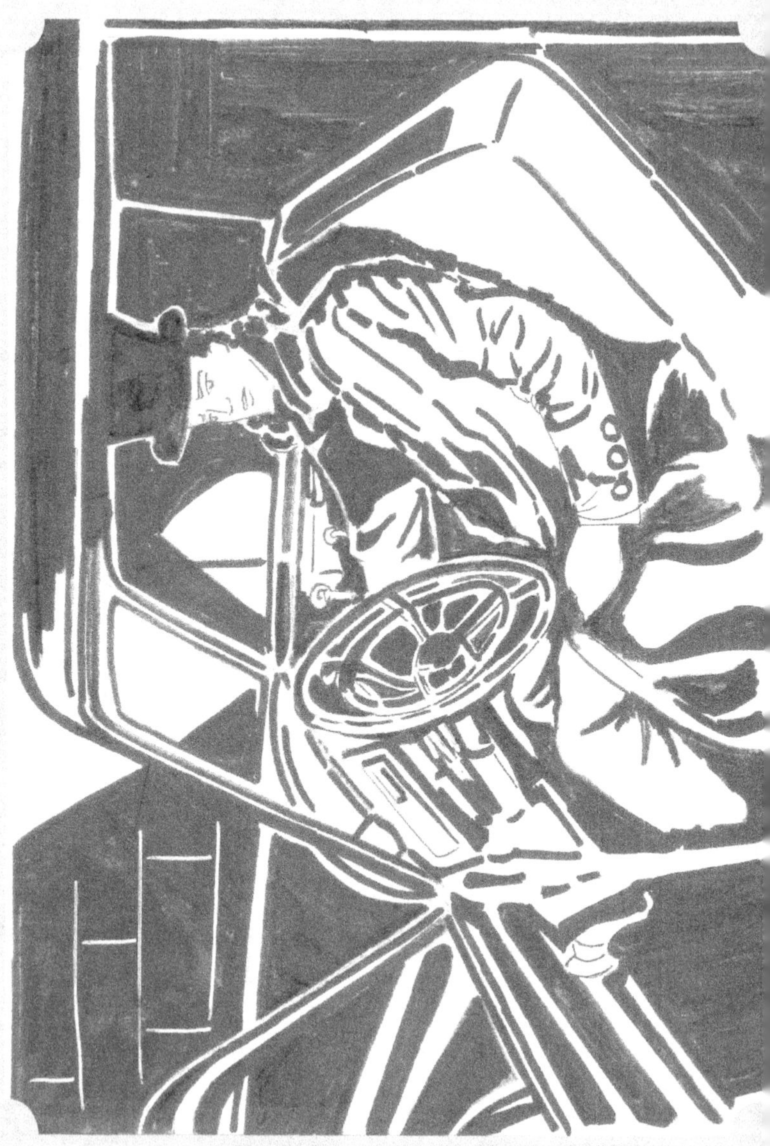

Mr. Ives: I was spending nearly 10 hours on a daily basis with well-dressed, beautiful, calm beings. Somehow, I started feeling safer at cemeteries than at pubs and other entertainment venues, where I would constantly be judged because of my old clothes and lack of dressing sense

Mr. Ives: There was this one funeral service where I couldn't hold back my tears as it was so damn emotional watching the family members bid farewell to their beloved grandmother.

It reminded me of how I used to spend my time after school with my dearly loved grandma. That's when I decided to leave a little note beside her grave right before the undertaker placed her six feet under.

Mr. Ives: It was the best feeling ever. The fulfillment that I got, I wanted more of it. As a result, I continued to do so for every funeral service that I was a part of. Every day after work, I would sit and write poems for the deceased so that they could read them in the afterlife

Mr. Ives: My walkman became my best friend. It would help me go on for hours and hours nonstop.

Mr. Ives: I often used to remember how my dad saved every penny he could to buy cassettes for his walkman, which all of us would listen to. Thankfully, I managed to save enough money to buy one for myself.

Mr. Ives: Somewhere between writing poems and listening to soul music nonstop, the seeds of artistry were sown.

Mr. Ives: Back to the discussion on why all the talented and brilliant musicians from around the country considered Tower Bridge as their gateway to a better life. On my way home from work, I was finally able to witness the awe-inspiring visual. It turned out to be exactly as Genine described.

It was a sight to remember. I was privileged enough to be able to witness the enigma on wheels. It was considered to be a vehicle of opportunity, the one that would help propel a musician's

career to a whole new level. It would pass the tower bridge every evening in search of the next big superstar. No one knew who rode the royal motor vehicle.

Lost it all

Mr. Ives: We are finally approaching the key plot. It was a fateful night; as usual, I was busy leaving notes for the beautiful souls resting six feet beneath when I heard heavy footsteps approaching the cemetery gates, the kind that would echo in the darkness, gracefully walking in a sequenced pattern. It was almost as if the ground was neatly marked for the footsteps to follow.

Mr. Ives: It was 3 AM and the clouds were as nasty as ever, with heavy showers. Upon turning to catch a glimpse of the possible danger impending, there emerged an entity that exuded poise and finesse. As godly as he appeared, there was nothing divine about him.

Mr. Ives: I was fixated on his personality, immaculate black attire, the kind that shoved away the pouring rain. Much to my surprise, he looked at me and smiled. His opening lines were, "God said, let there be light; and there was light. However, it isn't enough, for the darkness still prevails as an unavoidable curse'.

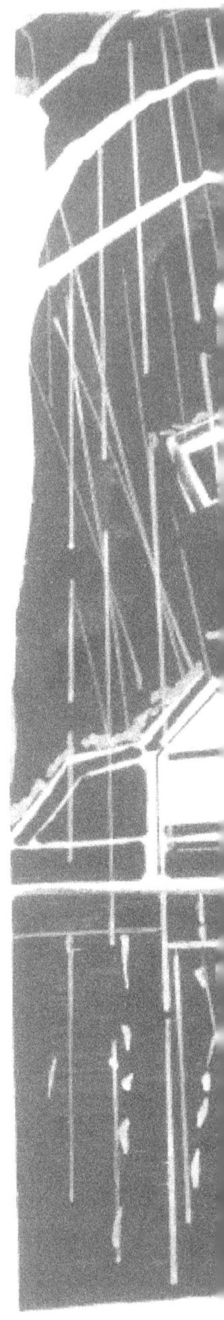

Mr. Ives: He continued, "You are in the right place if it is greatness that you are aiming for." As delusional as he seemed, I just couldn't resist the presence of the magnificent creature that stood before me.

He lighted up a cigarette and said, "Blessed are those gentle souls, the ones that are privileged enough to be going through your written notes." Damn! I thought to myself, how could he possibly know about this?

Mr. Ives: He sat right next to me and said, "This night marks the beginning of the rest of your life. Do as I say, and I'll make sure you become the person you were born to be. A Superstar! The kind that the heavens would desire and hell would preach."

Mr. Ives: To this, I reminded him that I didn't possess any special talent for him to nurture. I mean, I was a hearse driver for God's sake! Yes, I did intend to pursue music. However, I was clueless about it.

Mr. Ives: That's when he said, "You just have to follow my lead. Your weaknesses will become your strengths. And the thing that you love the most will make you a force to be reckoned with. The world will be at your disposal.

In return, you have to give me that one thing which serves as a gate pass to heaven. "I didn't quite understand, but I nodded and uttered the magical word that made him rejoice. I said, "YES." My only intention at that point in time was to explore all the possible options, as driving a hearse would lead me nowhere.

Mr. Ives: He gave me the address of the famous Apollo Theatre and asked me to enroll myself as a performer. According to him, showing up at the performance centre would seal the deal.

Mr. Ives: Before I could ask him any further questions, he began to march back to where he came from. His final words were, "See you on the other side, kid."

Mr. Ives: As instructed, I showed up at the Apollo Theatre. I wanted to make a good impression, so I decided to put on my work uniform, the one which I wore while driving the hearse. That was the only tux I had. I am not sure what happened next, as I completely went blank thereafter. I think I put on a show for the audience as my name was on the performer's list.

Mr. Ives: There was a huge lineup of performers, all well known in the club circuit.

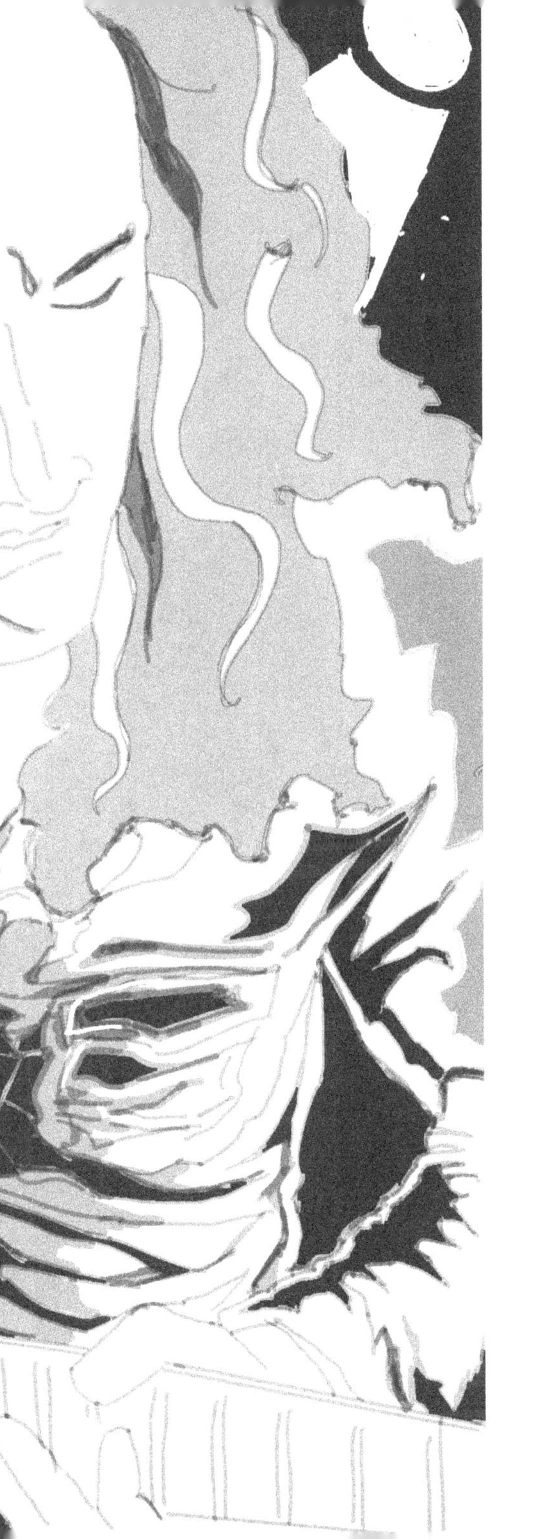

Mr. Ives! Madam wants to have a word with you!

I remember people applauding; however, it still wasn't clear as to what exactly happened back there. I might've been good, as something unbelievable happened right after that.

The very Automobile that used to take turns around the Tower Bridge stood right at the entrance of the Apollo Theatre. The minute I came out, the lady behind the wheels called my name out loud, stating that there was someone who was eager to talk to me. She was straight out of a beauty magazine!

Consider this the beginning of the
rest of your life! Come and see me
at my palace, The Priory of Atua, at
3 A.M., right when the moon is over
the River Thames.

Mr. Ives: As I approached the vehicle, she instructed me to have a word with the one who was seated at the back. I opened the door and there, lying in the back seat, was an enchantress, something that my eyes had never seen before.

That was when I learnt that I was in the presence of an unearthly being. A Goddess if you will. Although there was nothing divine about her. She gave me the most twisted instructions ever. I was asked to visit her palace at 3 AM, right when the full moon was up in the sky. If I time it right, the world will be at my disposal.

Mr. Ives: I will never ever forget that gorgeous yet terrifyingly scary night. I rushed home in order to get changed while keeping an eye on the moon to appear.

I borrowed my neighbor's ride; it was 2:40 AM already. I had just 20 minutes at hand. Life tends to test you by putting up challenges in different shapes and forms right before it presents you with opportunities. That's exactly what I learned!

Mr. Ives: I decided to pack my journal and kick start my journey to a brand new life, which was just minutes away.

Mr. Ives: Something about that moment changed me. I became kind of less conscious about myself. I started feeding off this brand new energy which I never knew existed within me.

Mr. Ives: I was finally able to witness the beauty of the River Thames. It was a once in a lifetime visual to see the moon shine right at the centre of the water body.

Mr. Ives: Finally, I made it right on time. In front of me was this massive mansion straight out of a haunted movie scene. There was something about it that I just couldn't stop starring at its unmatched artistry, scary yet beautiful.

Mr. Ives: There I was knocking at this massive door, not sure what to expect as things had been taking shape way too quickly.

Mr. Ives: After a couple of knocks, there appeared a tall, bearded man, inviting me in. His words were, "Congratulations on making it on time, lad". I was clueless as to what was going to happen next, so I reluctantly stepped inside the house.

Mr. Ives: I was asked to turn right and follow the path down to the waiting room. As I turned towards the hallway, the first thing I saw was this huge wall art, some sort of an album cover, which I came to know later on. We will get to that. I was literally in awe! It was breath-taking, to say the least!

Mr. Ives: As I continued to walk, there emerged wall art after wall art, all arranged along the passageway; it appeared as if I had entered some sort of art gallery, the one that would feed on your inner dark side.

Mr. Ives: The entire section of Girl on Girl art was the highlight. There was a special mention of the genre of erotica. She was the one who legitimized and legalized the genre and was now capitalizing on the demand.

Mr. Ives: The ones that sold the most copies were put up on the walls.

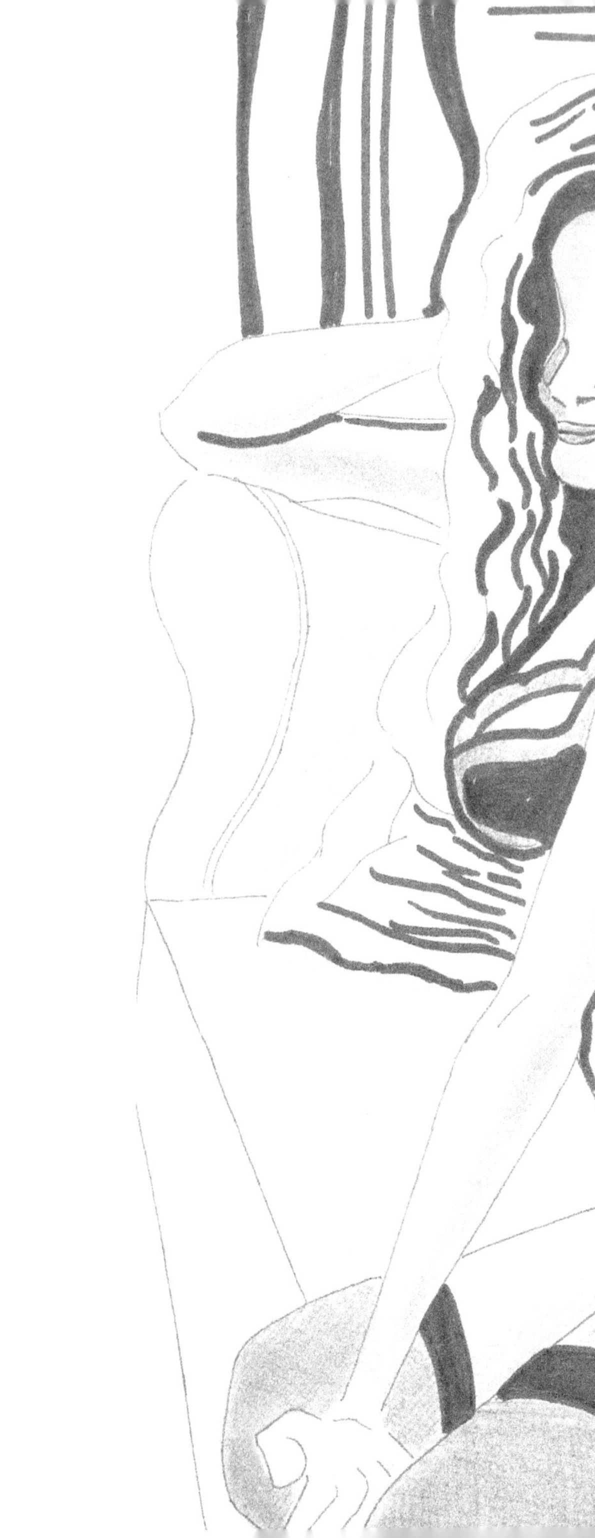

Mr. Ives: After walking for nearly 5 minutes, I finally reached the end of the passageway. As I turned towards the waiting room, I saw something that no one on God's green earth would have ever witnessed.

It was the most enchanting sight I'd ever seen, one I'd remember for the rest of my life; she was seated in the adjoining room, surrounded by ladies eager to be at her beck and call. She looked different from the last time. I was asked by one of the ladies surrounding her to wait outside till Madam was done changing her attire.

Mr. Ives: A couple of minutes later, I was allowed to enter the same room, which was full of ladies. Only this time there wasn't anybody inside except her. She looked utterly ravishing and different from the one that I saw earlier. She seemed to be illuminated with some sort of a divine sparkle, or rather an unworldly light, if you will.

Mr. Ives: She welcomed me with a smile and asked me to be seated on a sofa, which was placed right in front of her. As I approached the couch, gloomy lights turned on, revealing a massive wall mural depicting a performer with a microphone. The visuals were stunning, to say the least.

Mr. Ives: As I sat thinking if this night could get any crazier, she started walking towards me, asking about the painting and if I liked it. Of course! For me, it was a resounding yes! To which she said, "Good." Because it was none other than the future me, the one that she envisioned after watching me perform at the theatre and handing me a contract, the one that I ended up signing!

Mr. Ives: Upon signing the contract, there emerged a towering personality, the kind that could break you in two like a twig!! I was astounded by his size! Much to my surprise, he was introduced as my bodyguard, Belial! According to her, I was already an asset and my safety was her top priority. Things started to get serious in a matter of minutes!

Mr. Ives: While being introduced, I somehow happened to recollect one of the radio shows where an RJ was talking about how one man alone was responsible for ending the careers of 10 wrestlers, causing reckoning in the world of professional wrestling. He was none other than Belial!

Mr. Ives: Our first task was to put a band together; we were to be a 5-piece band, with a rhythm guitarist, a lead guitarist, a bassist, and a drummer. Of course, I was the lead.

While the other members were on-boarded pretty quickly, as Genine herself was a lead guitarist and a rhythm guitarist was picked up from the Apollo Theatre, the biggest challenge was to find a drummer. For which we turned to the local scene and came to know about a guy who would play drums in his garage, attracting a fleet of crowds. His name was TJ. He was a mechanic by profession and a drummer by passion.

Mr. Ives: In just a week's time, we started working on our singles. Before I could even react to the situation, I was already surrounded by cameras. I was living the life I'd always imagined, with DOPs doing their thing, directors arguing with the production team, and sets being built in accordance with the theme of the music videos. We had already cut multiple promos!

Mr. Ives: They used advanced technology to catch the minutest of elements, making sure that our promos looked picture perfect. There was this one time when they decided to shoot a rain sequence, and my God, it looked breathtaking on the screen.

Mr. Ives: We began our country wide tour and were credited with being the country's first band ever to sell out tours merely on the basis of promos!!

Mr. Ives: The response was phenomenal, to say the least! Who knew that a boy from nowhere could sell out tours and be the lead of one of the country's finest bands?

Mr. Ives: I continued to capitalize on the letters which I once wrote at funerals. It was as if I had discovered a pattern to greatness! Things were pretty much going my way, until that fateful night!

Mr. Ives: As usual, I got to the studio to work on a few ad-libs. I stumbled upon a couple of flyers that were being finalized for our upcoming tours. Only this time, our overall presentation was different. I started to argue, as it was not what our band represented.

We were told it was a campaign that was planned in collaboration with the government. If you ask me, what appeared right there was a perfect plan to control the minds of the citizens as per the frequencies of the sound. Guess who were their test subjects? Me and Genine! We decided to resign from the label with immediate effect. I still happened to have one with me. Here you go! They are still trying to retrieve this from me ever since I resigned.

Retro
lifestyle

Bio: Mr. Ives: is an amalgamation of artistry in any and every form. He uses various tools to express his wildest yet most authentic thoughts, making him a master storyteller. Dancing, making music, and sketching were, are, and will always be his actual calling in life, and he will continue to integrate the three, just as he has done with this one. Refer to the QR code to unveil the surprise!

Discord QR

YouTube QR

Spotify QR

Instagram QR

Sketches from my Upcoming Comic Series